For my three kids - Ielan , Oliver & Ronnie

I hope this book brings you all as much joy as you boys bring me each and every day !

Love daddy

Harry Mc Goldie

Written by
Micheal Chering

Illustrated by
Kiran Akram

Meet Harry McGoldie

With two golden fins that went
splish and then *splash*,
there bounded a goldfish who could
swim in a flash!

He swam for miles and
miles, but in circles,
of course,
while his mind
danced around with
adventurous thoughts.

The thoughts of flying!
Like a bird
or a bat.
Or searching for cheese
like a mouse or a rat.

To run fast as a cheetah with spots on his tail

or embark on a journey out to sea and set sail.

Harry McGoldie began thinking out loud, 'til his voice traveled upward through the soft cotton clouds.

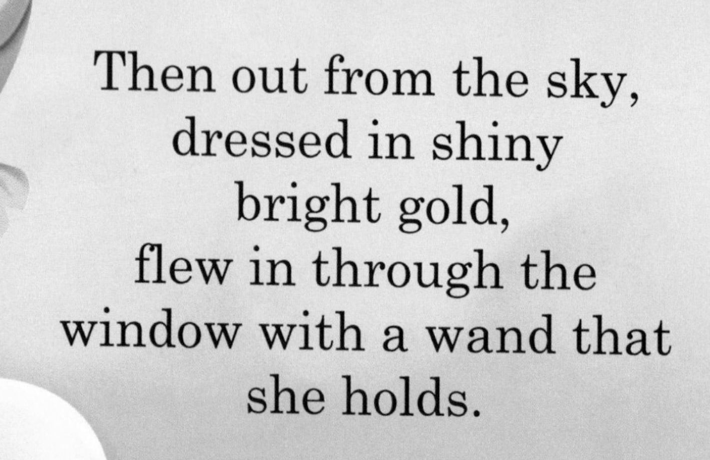

Then out from the sky, dressed in shiny bright gold, flew in through the window with a wand that she holds.

With a crown that sparkled on her
head like no other,
she described herself as his
fairy fish-mother.
"I will grant you these wishes for
you to explore."
Then with a *flick* of her wand, Harry was
one hundred feet from the floor!

Drifting and gliding,
he was soaring through
the air, until he was
spotted by a hungry eagle
at the fair.

Whizzing through Ferris wheels with
a grin on his face,
the hungry eagle took off and gave
Harry chase!

Trailing behind him with its razor-sharp beak!

"Help!! fairy fish-mother!" And with a *flick* of her wand, Harry started to squeak.

In the blink of
an eye, with a
sniffling sneeze,
appeared a
tiny mouse on the
hunt for some
cheese,

sneaking and
creeping around,
searching the floors,

ONLY TO FIND A BIG
GINGER CAT WITH
GIGANTIC CLAWS!

Harry jumped in
shock. "Oh, help!"
Harry cried.
The ginger cat stared
with its mouth
open wide.

Licking its lips, it
meowed, the horrible
beast!
Could Harry escape
from becoming its
feast?

The big cat pounced
toward Harry's tail!

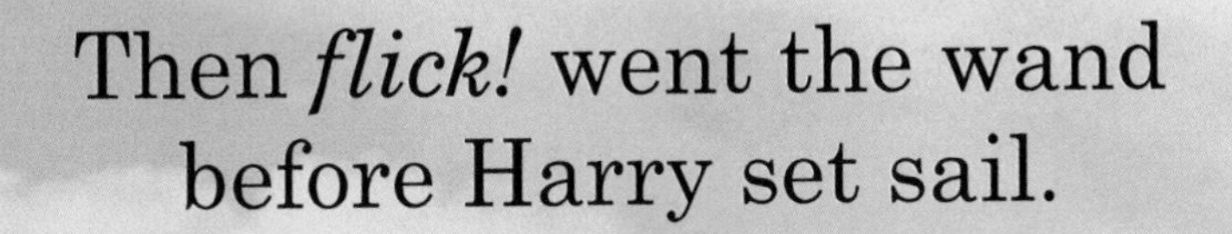

Then *flick!* went the wand
before Harry set sail.

At last, there was peace, safe away from all the threats,

no more hungry bird of prey, or mouse-hunting pets.

Harry finally found the freedom he was searching for, although . . .

Could there still be danger lurking just ten feet below?

Harry McGoldie was a pirate, sailing across the seven seas!

“AHOY, ME HEARTIES!” shouted Harry.

Then, with a huge THUMP! Harry buckled to his knees.

With another
THUMP!

and a
BUMP!

and a BASH!
and a CRASH!

Out jumped from the water
with an almighty
SPLASH!

This creature so great, so large, with teeth both big and bright!

went by the name of Bruce, the hungry Great White!

He thumped and
bumped some more
whilst snapping both
propellers down his
throat,

and after one last
thump, he managed to
snap half of the boat.

Harry called out loud
for help, with no choice
but to walk
the plank.

By now, he realized
after all how much
he missed his tank.

With a big deep breath, Harry
leapt out over Bruce's mouth
that was held open wide.

SPLASH he went into the
shark's mouth and back he
was inside . . .

THE FISH TANK!!!

"Thank you, fairy fish-mother," said Harry, "for showing me the way, I've learnt that all along, right here is where I want to stay."

Printed in Great Britain
by Amazon

79946032R00016